jarnal

VOLUME TWO

MASON JAR PRESS | BALTIMORE MD

Jarnal: Vol 2 is published by Mason Jar Press. The pieces have been published with the permission of their author. The authors retain the copyright for their work. Collection copyright © 2022.

All rights reserved, except for brief quotations in critical articles or reviews. No part of this book may be reproduced in any manner without prior permission from the publisher.

Cover design and layout by Ian Anderson.

This book is set in FF Meta Serif.

Published by
Mason Jar Press
Baltimore, MD 21218

Printed by Spencer Printing in Honesdale, PA.

Learn more about Mason Jar Press at masonjarpress.com.

EDITORS NOTE

Mixtapes. We all remember the fondly, especially for those of a certain cassette-and-CD generation. Those collections we made with a friend, or curated for a party, or devoted to a youthful crush. These kaleidoscopic expressions of emotion; camaraderie, excitement, love. They lived on as time capsules, while we grew and changed and matured, allowing us to return to a single moment in the past.

When I was tapped in May 2021 by my friend Michael Tager to guest edit The Jarnal, Vol. 2, the assignment seemed straightforward: put out the call, see what comes in, select pieces that seemed to capture a moment. And what a moment. We were all just beginning to come down from a year of a still-continuing pandemic and quarantine. We'd all had time to ruminate on life, caught in a little time capsule, reconsidering the ways we relate to each other. Surely in a world of amazing writers, I thought, this anthology would be an expression of that moment.

And then, fast forward a year to the spring of 2022, and submissions rolled in. The best pieces—those that make you go WOW—seemed to be ruminating on all points of life: birth and death, love and loss, leaving innocence behind and finding a new sense of self. Gone was any intention of having a single unifying theme or emotion. So how else does one make a mixtape?

These days, my mixtapes exist as playlists on Spotify. In January of each year, I make a new list, and over the course of the next twelve months, I drag-and-drop newly released tracks. These are never the pop hits, the mega-charters, the ten-million-YouTube views songs, but rather those little ditties from indie producers and basement rappers and Soundcloud nomads the algorithm pushes to me. The playlist is meant for home ambience; it's no longer a time capsule or a charting of my emotional state, it's simply to live and exist, knowing there's creativity out there in those underseen corners.

It's in this spirit I approached the Jarnal. In these pages, you'll find, instead, a journey of discovering the self in a chaotic world. These pieces range in manifesting moments from the deepest childhoods to the last breaths of life. Our writers, located around the globe, are speaking to themselves, but together, create a chorus of voices that strive to speak into existence those little moments of simply living and existing.

We're all just trying to make it to the next day, really. That's what I hope this mixtape of literature can be. Not something to calcify a moment gone; but, instead, be a constant testament to those emerging spouts of creativity that burst open somewhere on the globe, and I hope that with Mason Jar's algorithm of finding those readers who appreciate the weird and wonderful, we've brought that to you.

—Aditya Desai,
Guest Editor, The Jarnal Vol. 2

TRACK LIST

Bear by Meg Eden
page 1

What Happens When I Never Return, I Always Do by Caroline Bock
page 3

Four Poems by Tiffany Promise
page 6

Mama has passed on by Debra Stone
page 12

Wet Rot by Corinna Schulenburg
page 17

Supplements by A.C. Mandelbaum
page 19

The Field by Morgan Ziegenhorn
page 24

Girls Don't Shit by Letitia Despina
page 32

Four Poems by Taiwo Hassan
page 36

My Swan by Stuti Sharma
page 42

Four Poems by Ashish Kumar Singh
page 50

Two Stories by Kristen Zory King
page 55

Hunger Moon— by BEE LB
page 59

BEAR

Meg Eden

First thing I remember in Jillian's basement:
the bear on its hind legs, face frozen
to a grizzly growl, twice the height of me.

Against the green carpet & paneling, it looked
in its natural habitat. At its feet a plaque titled him
like an art piece, her father the artist.

Nine-year-old Jillian showed me his bar,
sat & downed an imaginary drink.   Behind her,
a wall of half-full bottles, empty glasses

on the counter. I'd never met anyone
who had alcohol in their house, let alone
a bar. A heavy stone dropped in me.

I asked if we could go upstairs, back to dolls
& trading cards. I forgot about the bear.
Only now, walking past her empty house,

do I think of it again.   Her old garden box
is grown over, the grass tall like cattails.
The kitchen awning's collapsed, garage door

open, hungry. Is that bear still in the basement,
forever dark & molding? The woods
are silent, sharp contrast to her father's

hunting days: his shots echoed loud like a cannon,

then silence. His dog's relentless barking.
My mother told me to come inside, said

he might mistake me for an animal.
I never believed that but followed her anyway,
our yard echoing with the nothing-sound

war brings. What's it like, to be
a hunter's daughter? The last time I saw Jillian
she had three earrings & smoked pot

in the school's back parking lot. I remember once:
a boy drove her down the street
on the back of his motorbike. I thought she might

disappear then, in the black
of his leather jacket. But that was not
when she disappeared. How absurd

it is for me to stand here now:
looking into her broken windows
as if I might catch a glimpse of her again.

As if she, like the bear, could be mounted,
owned & claimed,
a permanent fixture of memory.

WHAT HAPPENS WHEN I NEVER RETURN, I ALWAYS DO
Caroline Bock

The concert at the Kensico Reservoir in Valhalla is under the stars and free, and in the language of my father's parents. Yiddish. Crows darken the skies above the nineteenth-century earthen and gravel dam. The grass is moist. The clarinetist cradles the notes. Old ladies struggle up and dance by themselves. Everyone who's old sings along, everyone, even Pop. I didn't know back then that they were singing of loss.

I'm in the notes, flying. Twirling, whirling, a flock of one. I'm lying on my back on the blanket beside Pop, who's young, though I don't know that back then. He's in his red-and-white checked shirt, the scent of witch hazel swirling around him from his late-day shave. I'm not listening to the music; I'm doing what I do, daydreaming, twilight-dreaming, night-dreaming, nine years old and loving the wide-hipped, wide-open ladies dancing ever closer to us. *Bay mir bitsu sheyn,* the singer croons, and I turn to Pop and ask him what this means. I know he knows. I've heard him argue with his parents in Yiddish, this language of extremes—of screaming matches and whatever *this is*—attraction, match-making. One lady winks, and then another at Pop, who nudges me softly off. *Find your brothers and sister.*

Weeks later, Pop blares a hardcore military marching band LP. His turntable and speakers are positioned in the backyard by the blossoming cherry tree—the whole yard in New Rochelle grasps at the ripeness of summer. The yellow extension cord snakes through the grass that someone, me, the oldest, should cut. He's combating the neighbor's kids, who rip at guitars and drums in their double-car garage. Those neighbors have a two-car garage and a swooping, curved driveway. An in-ground swimming pool. A father and a mother. I don't know their names, but back then, I didn't think it odd. No one wanted us or our bad luck. No extended family visited. No old friends. This evening, Pop pumps the music. *The 1812 Overture*. The next day, used syringes will be dropped by the blueberry bushes that divide our yard from theirs. He orders us to fight back now, making us roar with laughter, making us strong. *More music,* says Pop. *The cannons at the end of the 1812 Overture—full volume.*

One day, I'll have a daughter who will play the clarinet. She'll reveal that a song of her middle school spring concert has a special name, *klezmer*, telling me like it's something new.

I don't know why Pop insisted on the concerts. He worked ten to twelve hours a day. I don't know how he did it without a wife and with four kids. He taught me words in Yiddish that mean the opposite of one another: *Schmuck. Mensch.* He told me to stay; he needed me. Then to go. In English. *Go.* He could be both a schmuck and a mensch.

Back then, he didn't know that I'd never return. Yet, here I am, and he's dead, and I am always returning.

In Syracuse, at university, I have a burnt-blond lover, who rows crew and collects butterflies flat in glass cases. He has me listen to his ropy, bare chest while he sings opera. German. Wagner. He doesn't know the words hurt because they are like Yiddish, but are not. He holds me absent-mindedly against the lyrics, wanting to impress me. What's lost is near.

I look up what the words from the old Yiddish song mean—*Bay mir bitsu sheyn: To me, you're beautiful or lovely.* Pop, you couldn't tell your nine-year-old those words? Out of loneliness or longing, I squawk this song, off-key, to the crow on the treetop in the park across from my home outside D.C. The crow knows the words and caws back. Bird-song. He's watching for me and alerts others—the sparrows and cardinals and blue jays; though when I appear with the birdseed, the crow keeps his distance, a symbol of death, and also for me: resilience and independence.

When I move to Queens weeks after college graduation, I have another lover. I tell this one: at night I become a black-winged bird, a kind of girl-crow, and I like klezmer. I don't cut the grass until it's knee-high. I dream in the day and twilight and night. I was raised by a Pop who brought me to free concerts and was partial to the *1812 Overture* with cannons at the finale. I grew up with nameless neighbors, but I like old women who dance like they don't give a fuck if anybody's watching. I want my future daughter to play the clarinet; and once, I had a lover who sang German opera and pinned butterflies behind glass—and this lover says: *to me, you're pretty. Don't go.* While some part of me wants to leave, I stay, for now.

MOTHER)HOOD
Tiffany Promise

born—slick & glistening—
wee nose, a shock of cat-black hair,
ten & ten, regular as regular
                                        as regular

but—unbeknownst—something left behind:
not another bb, no, just a sac sliver

i hemorrhaged for days
                    //then weeks

through unders, granny pads,
jampants, fitted sheets, straight to mattress
  into core

w/as little as a sneeze(welcome to

till an ultrasound found a shadow   of a shadow

so's

they scraped
clean. *As a seashell.*
    [ ] had to call and call

the post-procedure french toast
a cement mass in my throat/
wobbly, but brave, i pumped
& dumped for 24/went

to the holiday fest at P's preschool/
struggled-sore to make glitter
dreidel/cottonball snowmen/
pose for santa pics/etc

no one knew i was the emptiest thing imaginable:
overturned milkcarton<>brokenegg

                                                            (CHAFF)

whilst the wee one slept
strapped to my chest—elvin booties+mitts—
oblivious to the entire blip   ::bless::

her mouth a'suckle/my tit a bone
maraca-womb rattled w/every ouch

until i realized
  a'sudden
that i'd always always been rehearsin'
                    —disasterfuckinready, no doubt—
just a big ol' bag of scar ladders & foreshadow slits,
my body my (mothers body
regular as regular
                          as regular

SHOTGUN

Tiffany Promise

your Cadillac's still in the drive four long years later:
beached whale of a sun-bleached beast/*motherf'n Cadzilla*—
the darkest tint you can get in Texas w/out getting ticketed
bereavement bureau says there's an early termination fee
so we just let the lease run thin, thinner, thinnest/as if

your absence isn't enough

hitched an interstate with Grandaddy when I was six
his candy apple Caddy matched his gator-skin boots,
his leisure suit/stopped midway for *refreshments* at a road-
side juke/Crown & Coke for the old man, a Shirley Temple
for the little girl/bartend taught me how to knot a cherry stem

w/just my tongue

Mama drove her mama's '75 Cadillac to high school
a glossy pink dream machine that all the other girls envied
wasn't enough that she was Head Cheerleader, Miss Pearland
Oiler, bottle-blonde w/out the bottle/she also had that car
& those *titties* & was somebody's girlfriend
but not yet anybody's mother

someday I'll climb inside your stand-still Cad/pop the box,
peak 'neath the seats/find that beloved bling you inherited
from your buddy that got shot/poems I wrote in jr. high about
fro-yo & cute boys & the fort we built in the woods/maybe
even that long-lost recording of you singing *Weenie Man* or

your car keys

we'll hitch out to that juke joint off 290/drink Shirley T's &
shoot the shit 'til daybreak/Grandaddy'll tell a joke/Mama
will reapply her lipstick/you'll laugh so loud that I'll feel it
in my chest—*I won't ever let you go this time*—we'll bless Cadzilla
for having windows so dark that we can't see where we're going

or where we've come from

BREATH

Tiffany Promise

Today, when I turned on the faucet, ants poured out
    & peppered the tub. (chitin/porcelain) I thought
    of you, tiny tough guy, sticking your fist
    into any teeming anthill, saying,

They don't bite if you hold your breath.

But I could see the pink welts pebbling your wrists,
    hear your deep sleep scratching // tiny puss-filled
    bumps'd disappear in a few & you'd be set to dip
in again: Brave-faced plucky ducky turning blue as six-
thousand six-leggers spit venom into your little kid skin.

After you passed, Mom sprinkled you all over: ponds,
    stumps, creeks, fields, flowerbeds,
pastures, pits. (ash/earth) I hope the ants
    found you —used you— to build their hills.

They don't bite if you have no breath.

2/23/22

Tiffany Promise

was the first day that i forgot/took a text from mom to remember/i was busy with pb&honey waffles, school drop-offs, dirty diapers, *stopbitingyrsister*s/birthday wishes to a dead brother eluded the everyday—shit, sorry—when you were born i was obsessed/my baby/first baby/watched like a hawk yr soft-soft spot/how it pulsated with every thump/5-yr-old fingers twitched to dip thru wiggly skin/to pet the puddin' of yr brain—that silent secret spot that even mama couldn't see—i sat on my hands to quell the instinct/busied them with yr baba, paci, finger-puppet-shadow-show/ we be beasts all the way down, bubba/beasts all the way dooowwwnnn.

MAMA HAS PASSED ON

Debra Stone

theater: *noun,* a construction or edifice for dramatic performances.

Here comes:

Aunty J with her good hair, now the color of a silver fox swooped over one eye like Veronica Lake, swings it as she enters like Beyoncé. Mrs. M with her Blackglama mink coat, a legend in her time, gives J the evil eye.

This is an Episcopalian funeral, no drama here.

> That is to say, there won't be any fighting, whooping, hollering or fall-out crying here.

As

Johnny Mathis sings Chances Are & moments later Sarah Vaughn contradicts Johnny with a song no one remembers the name. Mama's friends chatter & laugh, reminisce about old Northside, Rondo, eat the catered food piled on the rented tables—my sister & I, career women, too busy to cook. This is what our Mama wanted.

theft: *noun,* act of larceny; stolen

January

One week before my birthday, Mama died. My birthday, always stolen; three weeks after Christmas everyone's broke. Wait until spring Mama would say, you'll get your present then.

You're so self-centered, said Sister.

At the age of three sister was lost at the Northside parade, the police man asked her, what's your mama's name? Mama, she said.

I sat by Lake Bemidji, sketching the willow tree. The leaves smelled like grass & the Mallard Duck with his emerald crown bobbed in the water while waves lapped on the shore. The willow tree, its thick branches with bark like varicose veins stretched over the water. I remembered, on a rope swing we jumped into Bassett Creek, the willow branch broke. Sister hit the water; the branch fell on her head. A drowning person makes no sound. I jumped in, grabbed her by her hair. Dragged her to the bank. She sat up and shivered & I gave her my towel. She never told Mama.

Melvin Stone circa 1948 Sumner Projects
North Minneapolis, Minnesota

Thelma Price on 814 Rondo circa 1947

Caption: Married November 12, 1950 St Phillip Episcopal Church

On the right, the former 706 Rondo Avenue home of her Uncle Turner. Mama's family house was several houses down but no photo exists. Brothers, Joseph & Turner, were very close and my mother played with her cousins like brothers and sisters.

theism: *noun*, belief in the existence of a god or gods.

In the underworld Mama refuses Hades & his wife Persephone. She was never one to obey. Just ask her husband. Dad said she made Father Brown delete "obey" from their marriage vows.

Scandalous in 1950.

They were scandalous: A North Minneapolis boy from the Sumner Projects marries a bougie Saint Paul girl from Rondo Avenue; places buried in cement now. He'd ride the University Avenue streetcar with Fanny Farmer. Fudge & roses, their courtship. Daddy Joseph said bring my girl home by 10 pm young man.

Daddy Joseph was not playing.

Octogenarian friends, women, a few men, struggle in deep snow, bone-rattling bitter cold, with walkers & canes through doors, still tough not defeated by death, to bid Mama farewell. They no longer drive.

Their children bring them, or the metro mobility bus.

cremate: *verb*, reduce to ash.

Cremated remains are pulverized bone, the body reduced to 3-7 pounds. I didn't want this writing to be about Mama dying of cancer infecting her lymph nodes, the breast, then the entire body in five years.

Things Mama disliked:

My 1970's Angela Davis Afro.

My "borrowing" her lingerie, sweaters & sneaking them back in the drawer.

Rolling my eyes.

Sassiness.

She didn't harbor many dislikes.

When I lived in Senegal for a three-month sabbatical she called me every Sunday at 8pm. The phone would ring & the Senegalese operator would say with a pronounced French accent, it's your Mama, then remind me after we hung up—don't forget your Mama will call you next Sunday. Mama had never traveled outside of the United States.

Sometimes I listen to her recorded voice message on my cell phone, she says: hello, it's Mama...as if I don't know.

She rode on the back of Daddy's motorcycle cross-country for two months in the summer of 1994. They were still scandalous.

She took care of all the family dogs & cried with us when they died.

She considered herself a working woman: mother, housewife, bookkeeper.

She read everything.

She was my champion.

In anger, I once said, I'd never be like you. But I am like you, I look like you, sound like you, I'm tempered like you.

It's your revenge; you knew I'd be like you.

Her last night was a good one with the family surrounding her bed to say farewell. At 2 am the night nurse called to say, your Mama has passed. I knew this before she called. Mama's White Shoulders perfume floated into my bedroom & with a light touch to my cheek, said she was leaving.

WET ROT

Corinna Schulenburg

A potato shouldn't squelch
but listen to the sucking sound
as I pop the root, wet rot
oozing blue on my finger.

Soft rot, leak rot, pink rot.
Pretty tater-tots-to-be turn
solanine, bitter air, better
safe than sorry as the dead.

The dead: one by one down
the cellar stairs in a small town
in Russia. Only the little girl
lives. The last one dead left

the door open. Let the air
out. Drill the holes deep.
Beneath, the permafrost
coughs up her ghosts. Belch

goes the methane. Pretty
deer fall down. Pretty soon
is too late. Petty, but I wanted
a better morning. Doom-

scroll, rabbit-hole, we all
fall down. We all fell for it,
that fashionable despair.
Where there's a window,

there's a way. Open the night-
shades. Let the light in. Scrub
clean the firm skin. What can
we salvage? What we can save.

SUPPLEMENTS

A.C. Mandelbaum

If the manager plays Beatles albums on repeat, you might have one minute of happiness for every minute of shelving, which might keep you awake. It might even keep you from reaching the tipping point. I just work here; this is not my life.

Whenever Jake spills something, he says, "Don't mind me; I'm a little tippy." Jake doesn't work here. He's tippy at his house. Jake says why don't I listen to music while I am shelving, rather than between shelving minutes. It is because I am reading while I am shelving. My brain is occupied.

The other kids call it "stocking." I call it "shelving" because every item is covered with text, like an everted book. A very short everted book. Tonight I learn that puffins use their wings like fins underwater to swim. They use the same things to swim and to fly. Cereal boxes are the most informative.

Shelving is easy. You have time to listen to music for one minute between minutes of concentrated shelving. And the manager has never implied that I am unproductive. Shelving would be difficult if you were tippy, but it's easy when you're tipsy. You have time to learn things.

The FDA regulates nutritional supplements as foods, not as medications. I have learned this uncountable times.

There are alternatives available for pet owners who do not want to give rawhide to their dogs, whose digestion can be upset by it, but I haven't learned what the alternatives are because I don't have time to read ingredient lists.

Multivitamins containing iron should be kept out of the reach of children.

Fluorescent lights upset the body's natural circadian rhythms. I read that on an LED lightbulb box.

Jake says I should pay more attention to my surroundings, more specifically the other kids. He says this when he picks me up after work at three in the morning. He picks me up on foot. Neither of us is in any state to drive by this point, nor do we have cars, nor do we have drivers' licenses.

This is why I sleep at his house after work: I can walk there. I tell him I cannot pay attention to the other kids. I have to defend the state of my brain. The other kids are an assault on the state of my brain.

I've written, "This is mine," in Sharpie on my "water bottle" so I won't lose it while I'm shelving water bottles.

Shelving minutes are longer than normal minutes. A minute of happiness is not a lot of time, so I dive into a rainbow-colored stream of electricity to maximize each second. I can barely read while I'm shelving because I have to move my eyes between inventory items.

Jake says some of the other kids go to our school when it's not summer. He says there is a lot of drama going on among them. He hears them talking in the parking lot where he is waiting for me while I pee like a racehorse in the employee restroom. Then he tries to relay to me what he's learned while we walk to his house. I tell him to stop. My brain has no room for the drama of strangers. The streetlights are banks of LEDs, the sky is dark and non-fluorescent, and all of the shadows on the street are pixelated. The only animals awake are nocturnal ones: cats, whose retinas flash back the LED light, and rats, who darkly dart or creep, tiny shadows moving unevenly in my peripheral vision.

The other kids are seriously concerned that Max is going to come back some night and perpetrate a workplace shooting incident. That's what Jake tells me. I yell at him before he can tell me why. I yell that I have enough to worry about. I yell that he is "harshing my buzz." No one has ever yelled those words with as much unironic fury.

We walk silently. I text my mom that I've arrived safely at Jake's house even though I haven't. It is delivered silently.

Before I know it, fluorescent light is overhead again. It doesn't matter that its source is far away. Twenty feet of distance does not dilute the power of fluorescent light. Fluorescent light annihilates all time between intervals of fluorescent light.

Tonight the manager is playing the Rolling Stones. I listen periodically inside my electric rainbow.

I go out back for a smoke break. There is an LED over the door, only one, so the shadows are analog. A girl is there. She says she doesn't like cigarettes but it's the only excuse the manager will accept for taking frequent breaks even though it's illegal for kids to smoke. I tell her, same. We drop our cigarettes and estimate the time it would've taken us to smoke them before going back inside. The girl says it's not such a bad job. She says you can zone out. I tell her I don't know how to do that. She says I might have better luck sober. It is the longest conversation I've had with the other kids ever. I let the girl drink from my "water bottle." She says by the way her name is May and then laughs at herself. I don't know what for.

I am dragged from the electric rainbow by shouting. I wonder if Max has come to shoot us all. I don't know what Max sounds like, but the shouting sounds like an angry woman. I don't know if Max is a woman. Sometimes the manager is an angry woman. I think these things as I walk swiftly through the warehouse—the other kids call it the "stockroom"—and out the back door.

I wait a cigarette's length of time and go back inside. There is no shouting. I peer cautiously around the corner of shelves looking for puddles of blood. A boy glances up from where he is squatting and lining up organic quinoa and looks back down.

Later, I tell Jake that someone was shouting tonight. He wants to know what words they were shouting but I'm not sure. I think "get out of here" and "go away." Probably just a wino trying to get in, he says. I ask him if "wino" is a word we say.

Cigarettes burn much faster when you smoke them than when you don't. May says that the secret to zoning out is to stop resisting. I think if I stop resisting I will start tipping. I don't tell her that. She wouldn't know what I meant. I tell her, "If I stop resisting, I will fall down." She says try coming to work sober.

I come to work sober. The fluorescent lights are flickering, all of them. The electric rainbow is inaccessible. The manager is playing music so bad it disappears into a large hole I didn't know I had in the center of my brain. I am shelving nutritional supplements. I remember an old movie in which someone carved "I'm eating my head" into a school desk. I find

May and ask her to go on a smoke break with me. She says she just went, but she comes anyway. The manager doesn't pay that much attention.

"I don't know how to stop resisting because I don't know what I'm resisting," I tell her. "Maybe eating my head."

"You're strange even when you're not drunk," she says, raising an eyebrow. "Just zone out. Relax. Don't try to fight the boredom. Don't try to remember things or tell yourself stories. Don't look at the clock. Don't think about what you're going to do before work tomorrow. Don't think, 'Someday this will be a distant memory.' The store is all there is and all there will ever be." She smiles.

"I don't like that," I say.

"Succumb," she insists.

"Last night I think I might have been hoping to find puddles of blood in the aisles," I say.

"What?" she asks.

"Not really," I say.

May says that Max got fired for shoplifting.

"Is it still called 'shoplifting' when we do it?" I ask.

May shrugs.

I am shelving granola bars. I think about not thinking all of the things I'm not supposed to think.

"I have a serious problem," I tell Jake when he picks me up.

"What is your serious problem?" he asks.

"My job is boring," I say.

"That is not a serious problem," he responds. A block later a rat is lying on its side twitching near a storm drain in the pixelated shadow of a tree. "That rat," Jake says. "It has a serious problem." The light is insufficient to reveal if the rat is wet or covered in blood.

"When I'm not at work, all I do is think about how I have to go back to work at some point," I say. "That rat is close to the end."

"You lack perspective," Jake says.

"Max got fired for embezzlement," I inform him.

He already knew that. "Stealing," he says.

The manager is playing the most beautiful music I have ever heard. Slotting items correctly is an engaging puzzle, like Jenga, Tetris, and Sudoku all rolled into one. I shelve within an electric rainbow of boxes of fluorescently illuminated dietary supplements. The FDA regulates them as foods, not medicines. They do not need proven efficacy for approval; they only need to not kill you at the doses at which you are likely to consume them, like marshmallows. These boxes teach you what people seek: serenity, joint health, cognitive support, reduced inflammation, a good night's sleep, stress reduction, enhanced immune response, vitality, healthy digestion, overall wellness, detoxification, blood vessel relaxation, elevated mood. This is what people seek, but all they get is life.

On the other hand, sometimes things work as advertised.

I am paying attention to my surroundings.

I take a smoke break after what I think is a long time. May says I can't smoke that here. I say I am in fact smoking it. She says I'm going to get myself fired. I hope not.

THE FIELD
Morgan Ziegenhorn

1.
I talk about tailgates like they're made
of iron arguments, for sitting
up and stars we sat there and you
asked me what next. I don't know
myself as well as I know your lips, it would
be easier to kiss you then to write
an essay about it. I wish we'd known, or known
more. You had a dream about high school, and
it was warmer at dusk and colder
when the sun was out, but you've never made
much since you dropped off the map
and hid in a cornfield. Dust. Train tracks past
you ask me what next and the bugs are humming.

2.
You ask me what next and the bugs are humming
birds but they aren't bright. The night sweats
around us like a quilt with dusty
secrets. Wouldn't it be nice to hide
what's next but you tell me since airplanes
have been invented you don't trust
flying and I don't see hummingbirds
just giants with buzzing wings and
metabolisms, the twilight robbing them of
their daybreak colors, you don't want to
go anywhere red or blue. One time
I saw a seal in a pond off the window
of a train, of thought, and it was just car tires
I'm tired, and we're sharing a cataclysm.

3.
I'm tired, and we're sharing a cataclysm
of what next do you remember how we
met, at apocalypse survival class and I
taught you how to spell it because you wanted
to be a writer, the world was bigger then
it was small again, I never mastered laundry
before we fell off the map. I thought it wouldn't
matter if we dried all the matter if we
had fluidity between us, just two strangers
with a lot of history, to anyone else it looks
like teenage spirit in the moonlight,
it looks like cutoffs and the quiet, it
looks like rain, I look like hell, you smell
like heaven falling, like everything else will.

4.
Like. Heaven falling. Like. Everything else will
be weather then, feathers and angels and rain mixing
(muddy) (fallen) (wings). We're holding our
arms touching. If we keep looking up
we'll catch them in a net of not speaking, the night
creeping onward with a southern drawl. Minor
feathered bruises I won't tell apart from
my normal ones, from my small hatred
of small towns, from me to you spit
and handshakes in the field, nose full of dust, you
ask, the answer is what next but the shape
would surprise you, like feathers for nets
of arms, swirling air resistance, like the sound of
an airplane made of angels made of dust and mud.

5.
An airplane made of angels made of dust and mud

(crash) into the field, or somewhere else. I've barely
traced a map as long as your hands, you speak
of breath, of what comes next. Of your
life in the field of train tracks and quilted
secrets of sticky summer, if we ever get
out of this field I'll tell you of my small
love of small towns, my own quiet
abusively purpling the parts of me
I hide in the field but come back because
it's free. Lie next to me and we'll watch the rain feathering
down the headlights. You say you'd like it better if it was
less about a tail, humming, wanting to spell out
in a story about fried chicken and Joo-lie.

6.
In a story about fried chicken and Joo-lie,
lie down, what next, maybe I can just
show you a way without roadmaps
where this town doesn't even show
up just a puddle next to the lake
of rocks, dried town in a ziplock baggie of
crashed fields where teens lock lips on a
tailgate in trucks deserving of love, which drives
better than they can, headlight's out,
or you just turned it off, or I don't care
or if you didn't I would've anyway, or
I'll fuck you, or it doesn't matter either.
You ask what next. Raining layers. You spell
what comes after I love you.

7.
What comes after I love you
in some dusky dust dictionary we didn't use
in high school and someone ripped

out the entry about humming, about birds.
Don't touch. I just don't know if I could
ever be. What next. You expected to love
a girl like me anyway. Some roads are
unexpectable, words that don't exist spell
(wingsical) (rainsitory) (cornication)
the truth, you would've spent
more time in class but you were in
the field, lost in the field, plowing or
something I never learned to do was trust
a farmer's tan or whatever was under it.

8.
A farmer's tan or whatever was under it,
under rainstorms, you spelled wrong like a
(dusty) (sticky) underline. A burning
sparkler. No, not really, something
more heroic. A broken crown. A meta
morphosis. Yeah I'd still like wings. Yeah
I love you like I pretend to. Yeah I'd pull
my own skin off if it would tell me what was
wrong with me. You don't give a flying fuck
for flying, for tails, for what next, you want to be
blue. You count cataclysms with your eyes
closed. You kick the tires, birds fly out humming.
I've always loved red boots. I wasn't made for
walking. I wasn't made for I wasn't made

9.
walking i wasn't made for i wasn't made
from only carefully crafted feathers and i can
morph but not as much as you said you would
try to once the apocalypse was over
nothing crawled under my skin anymore

you got us stuck you got us into
a cataclysm this field and we haven't seen
a crash or sense i could rip open i want to
i thought i would recognize more than the big
dipper or at least find Orion in a field you're
sick of having sex you want to meet
other hummers, other tired bobbing
tires in the lake, bobbing with fried sense, bobbing
like progress, bobbing for survivors

10.

Like progress bobbing for survivors
at the last event we went to, we asked what
next everyone thought we looked dusted
apart, but you sort of looked like an
angel but that's what they meant. You wish
all shirts had the American flag suffocating
heat or fried chicken with whatever that seal is
that crashes symbols, the star spangled
humming bangled byrd and you were embarrassed
by the schism and that I spelled it wrong, but that
was sort of the point of this whole party
cataclysm, that was Orion, or the broken crown, or
the way the sky swirls at dusk in the field and the
trees look like power lines look like pencil marks.

11.

Trees look like power. Lines look like pencil marks
the space between us, stars I can't handle
pretending to give a shit about our third
world, the first being Eden and the second
the Wright brothers, the third I call ours because
we're the only sparklers left, the only hummers
bumming it out in the field, the only headlight's

broke, you fix it, you ask what next, you
want to be useful in a way an angel couldn't
wing it, it's too sticky I can't bear to peal
out an I love you, or seal myself into a canteen
of dusty Sundays or even a white address to
appease your mother's cadaver locked away, burnt up
in the dusted dusk the wings of even angels blind us.

12.
In the dusted dusk, the wings of even angels blind us.
Someone's humming about rainstorms, someone
knows we lost our tree in Eden, running
and running in the marsh, someone's
feathered with a sparkler in the parlor, burning
the right way, Wrights writing about how
rain looks from above us, they saw us in
the field, they left us there because you
wanted to know what next I'll peel us
open like a tire rind, I'll do anything to
learn to spell, the rim of the cataclysm, trying
to balance or at least not to be ill I'd kill it if I were
you, if I knew you, if you wanted me too and we're
hurtling towards (the field) an apocalypse.

13.
Hurtling towards (the field) (an apocalypse)
we could follow it east to the tree where
I wish I hated myself as much as you
we're supposed to do at least something with
secrets, with lines, with pencil marks the spaces of this
small town I could careless touch, would you even let
me, if you thought about me at all. I know it's about
this truck and fuck this heat and the dust
moves inside of us but it at least stays

through sunset. We thought the world of each other
would end, heaven falling to get away from this
cataclysm, two stars are moving together too fast in
the field, I can see it, you ask where, you don't look,
I'm begging and begging you to turn over.

14.
I'm begging, and begging you to turn over
so I can face the feathers, the humming in
the lake, someone's practicing in the
marsh, someone's barrel rolling on a horse
to get out of this field, this small town where flying
scares you like the tires, like quilting in secret,
you're a cataclysm, the apocalypse
fries chicken, the tired seal stops swimming
in the rain, the sparkles spin, the
dust bottoms out below us, you don't
know what next, you fixed it that way, your
head, lights out, field over, mud feathers,
I'm peeling, stars fly everywhere, and I talk finally,
I talk about tailgates like they're made.

15.
I talk about tailgates like they're made.
You ask me what next, the bugs are humming
I'm tired and we're sharing a cataclysm
like heaven falling, like everything else will.
An airplane made of angels made of dust and mud.
In a story about fried chicken and Joo-lie,
what comes after I love you.
A farmer's tan or whatever was under it
walking. I wasn't made for, I wasn't made
like progress bobbing for survivors'
trees look like (power lines), look like (pencil marks)

in the dusted dusk, the wings of even angels blind, us
hurtling towards, the field an apocalypse,
I'm begging and begging you to turn over.

GIRLS DON'T SHIT
Letitia Despina

i intercepted Otto on his way out of the house to the park because it was one of those days when i didn't know how to be alone. he had brought a blanket and we each read our books in a parallel sixty nine, like my grandparents used to sleep during winter when they shared a bed to save heating. i had written to Zed to say let's have beers in the sun and he had replied he's frustrated over his banjo-playing so he needs to go skate to blow off steam but i could join for a concert later if i felt like it. i felt like it, but delayed my arrival and had some beers as i was reading *leaving atocha station*, stumbling over this one sentence over and over again, "had the effort to prolong my adolescent experimentation indefinitely shaded imperceptibly into fearsome if mundane dependency? had mythomania become methomania?" i laughed out loud because i was, all at once, a true liar who was pretending (or do i want to say *trying real hard*?) to be some casual spring/summer collection version of herself, who just wants to be friends and to have fun (which was true & loud enough that i could hide behind it my feelings for this boy Zed, a new kind, not the boombox type, not the fascination fling, but an earthy-sort-of-wanting-to-get-to-know-him that i was willing to sit on and wait for to crack), while simultaneously trying to extend my adolescent experimentation beyond what i felt was appropriate, as evaluated by the import of authentic societal voices in my head, who wore ties to look serious and then used them to perform autoerotic asphyxiation when no one was around. why would i allow them in my brain, a fucked-up fragment of a fucked-up world, i have no idea.

i left the park, took out a hundred kroner at the ATM, fifty for a beer or two and fifty for the entrance to the place for this punk concert and then felt like i was ready to shit in my pants. i wasn't nervous, i meant this absolutely literally. so i hurried to find this place, i remembered there was a library on the same street that could save me from annihilating shame but suddenly there they are: the concert-goers, sitting at tables outside. i met Zed's eyes, froze but somehow kept going, said 'hi i got to pee' and brushed past, all in a supreme confidence that can be synthesized only from such deep embarrassing discomfort. the graffiti on the toilet door said 'er det det det er?' and i read it with such joy, *is that all there is?* almost palindromic in danish, a little victory of words in this constant 'failure of language to be equal to the possibilities it figures.' a little victory entrance for me, too, at least by appearance, which was enough, my only goal (besides that of hanging out with this boy) was to feel cool and calm and able to integrate and penetrate all make-belief strata of different music scenes.

after i sat myself on the bench beside him. surrounded by friendly punk concert goers, i was in my element without belonging to it, without committing to it, i didn't care whether or not i would be identified as a fraud, because i was openly one, and i was also genuine about my excitement of attending this thing. he was chatting with some folk, didn't pay much attention to me, which made me feel at ease, i could do my own thing, which was observing and also smiling to myself when our legs accidentally touched under the table.

every third person sitting or standing around there, outside this dirty punk place, smelled like piss and beer, but in a friendly way, one that went along with their outwardly, overall inclusiveness of non-punk-normative-looking-folk such as myself, and if this isn't true punk i don't know what is.

by the time Katinka made a spliff, i had finished a couple of beers, and when she handed it to me i imagined hearing the little beep beep of *approved! that* card terminals make and my relief was actually joy, just like when you buy something not knowing how much money is left on your account but you hear it and see it: approved! feeling that way and unaware of the strength of this spliff, i may have had one-too-many puffs, pushing adolescent experimentation well into that monday night of my thirties. when the concert was ready to start, i asked Katinka to lick her stamp and clone-stamp my wrist, which she did, laughing, and i, in spite of never having even tried to pull something like this off, just walked in, with such a trail of where-the-fuck-did-it-come-from-confidence behind me, that when i got asked to buy a ticket i showed my wrist schlepping this sloppy, vague trail of a stamp, the guy nodded and i was granted passage as well as, sorry bands who were playing, 50 extra kroner to buy more hancock beers. which i did, placing myself autonomously in that space, sending Zed the look of *totally awesome* when our eyes met over the room and i felt like his were asking me if i'm ok. i was more than awesome actually, i was the ruling planet of my monday night, all these fast riffs made my total transition into dedicated enjoyment, already re-familiarized with punk as i was from the previous week, when i had dropped by the hardcore festival, with my post-house-warming group of acquaintances-turned-friends. we got in for free because it was so late, and as we were slightly jumping and dancing someone announced there was some japanese hardcore band playing in the other hall so we all rushed out. this other room was huge and packed with people, and without aiming for it i caught sight of Zed's silhouette and went straight to him in a giggling frenzy, pulled his hair from behind, then i ducked and walked around him behind people only to appear on his side and pinch his cheek, catch his annoyed look, give him my warm regards naughty smile, receive his and then disappear into the crowd to Elena, to whom i announced my descent into the mosh pit. i was in it for the whole show, which probably wasn't so long, but enough to allow me to have this birds-eye view of myself, complete with an intervention from the tie-wearing-voices saying *who-mosh-pits-in-their-thirties, you kook?* but i took out my middle finger to them and to me, and emerged from that ebbing group pogo session with a straighter back and a joke to keep me smiling till today: i was having so much fun out there in that crowd of jumping and shoving because i'm so good at pushing people away.

and when that monday punk concert was over, i followed the group dynamics outside, new hancock in hand, drunker than i knew, so drunk that after five seconds of sitting next to Zed and unintentionally ignoring his question about my state of being, i stood up and confidently made my way again to *my* bathroom stall, where i carefully and maturely emptied the contents of my stomach for that post-vomit lightness. i returned to the crowd, sat next to him again, answered his question coherently, and listened in on the conversation, only to repeat step one ten minutes later. this level of going all the way on a monday night was a new peak, whichever way the gaussian curve goes, and when Zed announced he was going home i raised myself, grabbed more bags than i owned and said i'm coming with cause we're going the same way.

for the whole ride home i pestered him to let me ride his skateboard to show him what i had learned but all i got was no, it wasn't safe, i was drunk, it would be stupid, but i continued to beg and insist, some mechanism i had mastered in childhood to get everything i wanted from my mother and, inebriated as i was, forgot it is wildly inefficient, if not detrimental, in any forms of human interactions. we had a cigarette on his stoop before each going our own way, and even though he was earnestly annoyed with me and i was still enjoying this one-to-one, there was some kind of chemistry, imagined or real, who can tell, that i had enjoyed around him since we had met. i got safely to bed, took off all my clothes and put myself to sleep as any respectable adult on a monday night that contained loads of unreasonable fun and also some frustration: you know.

MÒÓMI

Taiwo Hassan

for my grandmother

every time the smell of camphor makes me a temporary home, i still hear the softness in your cackles filling these empty spaces on my palms and your frail hands tracing salvation on each line, massaging my qualms into dust. anytime your face is a puzzle in my head, i morph into old brooms, sour cherries, the moans in between a mortar and a pestle, i remember your blobbing veins on my mother's arms, how they've become feathers on my wings too, *mòómi*, do you watch me fly now? i want to hear a cuckoo's chirp and remember the songs you never completed, tread through a market and feel your hands firmly on mine, again. but what is grief if not broken pieces of a full mirror holding strange mixes of hope and regrets in their cracked reflections? i journey into several of your photographs and still find little prayers sitting, dusty. i call them flowering wounds, scanty scars, just blooms in disguise. i'm trying, i swear, i am, to lay these burdens down. but when the afternoon sun decides to bring you close and remind me what it means to wear your skin, i hold my breath and swim in your stories, dilute my blood in their richness & remember that place where it all began, that house that never went naked.

FOR LOST HOMES
Taiwo Hassan

here we go again, i begin this ritual
where i travel into my past,
asking myself if all my troubles also began
and ended with a prayer,
if [ ]   wasn't all my troubles.

i wondered why i had to be cut, why i   had
to be more less.   i once heard adorning
your demons with a noun fades their
colours. but tell me, why am i still blue?

the day i first drowned,

in familiar cracks/ on a drying face/ hollow hearts/ carry weights of the past/ years of woven wails/poured from these eyes/& my body/ dug for harmonies/ in every melody/ they could find/ as if to say/ they've always rebelled too/ as if to say/ silence is a song/ not only these lips know.

i jump these unmade fences, fully aware of their history, knowing there are only so many places a tree can look down on when it finds out its seeds are no stranger to your palms.
now, watch my scars unburn into fresh wounds.

for the fleeting days, the breezy evenings, the beans, onions and burning coals, the fusion of their aroma, and the raw innocence in the nostalgia they leave, i empty myself into this poem.

i want to rest on my mother's face and not feel guilt flowing into me, not feel this pool that lies moribund on her cheeks hold some weight, one a zephyr struggles to be a metaphor for.

i want to remember when squeezed *efinrin* and salt concoctions meant a morning well begun & how
in old brooms *asalam alaikum.* sour oranges
my skin learnt the art of elasticity, filling it with colours that's no stranger to this river my body houses.

i want to swim here, and not lose myself. but how do i teach joy how to float? is where the scent of freshly washed laundry and familiar lullabies replace this viscosity flowing in me?

see, my windows too, know how to usher the moon in, these big white rooms can be more than just bearers of familiar shadows, and these doors aren't another accent in the language of everything that sinks - i know this house,
can still be a home.

i know this can be a poem where each line
isn't any everyday wound i nurse,
and every rhyme, a scar that lacks the cover of healing,

where scattered metaphors aren't heavy *sujuds*
and spaces, *rukuus* that never butterflied into hope,

a reminder peace once
laid on my hands

and nestled on my face.

that love, once lived here too.

ADIEU,
Taiwo Hassan

the sun whispers to a yawning sky
and the clouds become its walls, fading
into heavy echoes, into
the wandering thoughts of a traveler,
into an àdìre scarf, vibrant despite.
black twinkles spread like flying stains,
flapping their webbed wings, as if to preach the gospel
that somewhere, even darkness can be some beauty.
is this where darkness too, becomes a testament
to many of its ironies?

somewhere in a moving bus, there's a man boy
watching his shadows dissolve into something vicious
& the more he peers, the more he tastes their
saltiness, is this
the elasticity he's crawled from all his life?
sometimes, the origin of a name is a wallflower
blooming in a closet, chanting, *blue boy bloom.*
still, farewells lazarus again, reminding tired bones
and hollow eyes that goodbyes are just sentences
without the miracle of a full stop.

the sullied words of an headline run into his eye,
then falls into his face, then a bruise in
his head, another scar comes undone, ashes unburnt.
this is another poem where metaphors
that have retreated into their Genesis
rear new heads, once again.
ina lillahi wa inna ilahi rajiiun.

he knows every drop of rain crawls back to the sky
but where are the two thousand and two reasons
to make sense of this one breakage?
there is a storm growing in his chest
and nothing is a salve, nothing, is close to a balm, nothing
carries the potential of growth except questions.

did he also hold similar clouds? if
those frail ribs of his found a way
to house the gray and the ground,
be the beauty   and the chaos, be the beauty
in chaos, would he have found peace
despite all those punctures? would
he have gotten any chance to fold
into what this poem began with.

ina lillahi wa inna ilahi rajiiun—From God we came and to him, we shall return.

THE NOISE
Taiwo Hassan

on mornings like these, the boy/ in a man/ journeys into his throat/ hoping/ to find a voice he once lost/ to call the *A'dhan* and not stutter. a mosque is once again a reminder of the things he could let out, and *wudhu*, a salve. diving into subhi feels like arriving at a market/ high hopes/ a mix of caution and excitement/ an open heart/ and running hands. he feels the stillness of the night sweep through him, its essence carefully picking his qualms apart, this is how he becomes another synonym for a pieced puzzle at every *sujud*. as he lifts his eyes, then hands and his almost dried lips to recite *suratul-ul-fatihah*, he tries, he prays those worries into dust too. he does his best to flow with the tides of each verse but a stone struggles to define his spirit. how do you tell willing wings to melt into the skies when each of their feathers is a testament of elements unburnt, of dreams undeciphered? perhaps today, this heaviness will melt into the colours of the ground as his forehead tastes its coldness. perhaps today, he too will be the subject of a miracle.

MY SWAN
Stuti Sharma

Fred only came over to complain about his dead wife because he wanted to ask me out for a walk as a guise for fucking.

It was raining that day too, also the day my cat turned into a sparrow. She had been out in the fields and the swans had started getting aggressive. One clamped her paw and wouldn't let go. I batted at the swan with my bare hands until it stopped, and its entire beak fell off. When my cat finally got away, I saw a trail of fallen beaks.

"Where do they come from?" I had asked my older sister, who had seen the storm clouds from a perch in a nearby tree.

"The swans' beaks fall off when they are yanked from holding on too long." She had told me, as I looked at the trail of charcoal-colored discarded beaks.

My cat had turned into a fragile sparrow, and it seemed like the swans had done a number on her. I looked down at her in my hands, feathers wet from drops of rain, and noted her beak hadn't fallen off. I felt relief.

The swan doctor came to the house and started to fuss over her. He pulled out his kit and had her strapped to a small spatula, a make-shift surgery bed. He asked me to hold it, and I was afraid. I've always been afraid to hold birds.

She stirred as the swan doctor stitched her wounds and applied salve. I marveled at how she used to be so big, the size of an opossum - a very fat, capable cat. How did she turn so small?

When swan doctor finished up, she turned into a bigger, dry cat. Her paw wasn't working at all right and her tail seemed to have been caught by the swans in the field too, but she walked around and happily munched on her bowl of food.

***

Fred arrived just as the rain started. We hadn't seen Fred in a handful of months. There was something of a stranger in his manner, but at the same time, something incredibly familiar.

The town was close-knit and Fred had arrived from the closest thing we had to a hub six miles away. He just lost his wife, and everyone was expecting a visit from him, an update on his life, a chance to feed and comfort him. Everyone was losing someone these days. His eyes swam with tears but he seemed content, able to see and hear about other things in the world other than blinding grief.

My parents adored Fred. When Fred arrived, all eyes were on him. They fed him warm soup and gave him piles of blankets on which to lie and tell his story about his wife. My mother seemed especially excited to prattle on her many successes in trade and business these days. Here were new ears to be impressed by her, to fill the void with her need to talk about herself. My father seemed happy to have someone to host, to marvel over his many dishes and new experimented flavors and spices. My sister did not care about Fred and eventually disappeared to some remote corner of the house to draw in peace. I was worried about the cat. My mother at some point had said how she wasn't worried about the cat because the cat did not like her and would make her feel unwelcome in whatever room she was in. But his eyes didn't look at me. I hated this about him, how when things were bad, his first response was denial. The cat was my cat.

***

Sunset was approaching in a few hours, and Fred got up to go.

Fred asked me, as he put his shoes on, "Do you have the rest of the day free to walk with me? Do you mind walking a few miles out?" I nodded. In my mind, I tried to play out a negotiation outside of Fred's idea of how the walk would go. He would wait until we were alone to give me new books, a reward for taking whatever it was he did to me. Maybe I would only walk two miles when he gave me the books and then turn back, unspoiled for once.

To get back home, Fred needed to catch the train in town by the end of the day. On urgent business he told us, pertaining to his wife's estate. My dad asked, "Are you sure you have to go? We don't have much space but I'm sure we could make accommodations for you in the girls' room."

"No no, I must go. The company of your brilliant daughter to the train station is more than enough!"

And I had some eagerness to walk with Fred, as Fred meant new books. Every time I saw him, he produced two or three new books for me and talked to me at length about their authors, their meanings, how I could extract inspiration for them for my own poems. "Maybe one day, I'll be giving your book to others," he had said once. The books always excited me, and I thought this excitement and the feelings that accompanied his eventual requests when he saw me must have no difference. I could only identify that I had a mixture of desire and then shame when it came to Fred, but mostly the warmth of companionship. I'd never met anyone before in our small town who had talked about the things I thought about.

★★★

Fred had taught the writing and reading classes I took in the small library next to the convenience store in town, the autumn of the year before this one. I'd loved how he read the first line of every book with reverence, like he was unveiling the first jewel in an ancient treasure box for us to admire. I fell in love with words, but I think Fred hoped I would fall in love with him. I was too young to know the difference. I suppose there was something alluring about him, this man with olive skin and dark hair, similar to that of mine and my family's—though we were varying shades darker—and pressed shirts, who spoke of poems like they were his old friends. But when he looked at me I felt a burning need to hide. The feeling was the opposite of the joy of reading a beautiful poem. I hadn't known that that feeling existed, having discovered its happier counterpart only two months before Fred started having me take "excelled lessons" which took place after the normal classes.

"Only for the best readers and writers," he explained. And, interestingly, I was the sole pupil who met this esteemed rank. That first afternoon, he poured us both mulled wine. He explained his wife made it every autumn from wild berries and then asked me to describe my response to the poem we focused on in class. As I spoke, his hands casually grazed across my thighs. The only thing between his touch on me was my cotton trousers. A gasp caught my throat. He asked me to read the poem again, and as I was reading I felt his fingers touch my neck very gently.

"No matter, your hair is just falling over the text so I can't see it." His hands followed my hair, across my shoulder, then up my neck. The wine made the touch feel electric. When his fingers reached my chin, he turned my face and kissed me fully. I'd never been kissed before. Something stirred in me. In one breath, it felt a sudden brightness, like wings growing between my shoulders. But in the next, the wings rotted and fell, like a bird hitting a window. The brightness sank to a dead weight in my gut.

"Did you feel that?" he asked.

I nodded and touched my lips. He tapped my lips. "Not that. I mean what you felt inside. Did you feel something new?"

I nodded, astonished at how Fred was smart about these kinds of things. How had he known kissing could cause something inside of you? Even with the poetry books I had devoured in the past few months, I surely could not have predicted that. Looking back, I wish I asked what he had felt, too. But I didn't. I thought only Fred was allowed to figure me out. I never realized I had already had him figured out from the start, from that first kiss. I stayed wide-eyed and silent as he explained, "That's poetry. That's where your poems will come from."

***

The next week, he bent me over his desk. Once he finished, I didn't have a moment to process the warmth down my leg, what happened inside of me, because he started talking right away. I had never seen that before. No one in my family had discussed what sex was, what the boundaries of sex were, who you did it with, and who you didn't do it with. It was agreed it was something people did to have children, to keep their shops open, their farms running with free labor.

He eyed my notebook. "Do you share your poems with anyone?" he asked, as he zipped his trousers, straightened the sleeves of my shirt and smoothed my hair. I shook my head. I had never let the notebook out of my sight, and Fred had never opened it. In the entire time I knew him, he never forced poems out of me. Every poem I read to him, every line that came to me that I was ecstatic about - they had been my choice to share. At least I had that.

"This is why I knew you were a special writer. The best writers were the ones who wrote from the hidden things, who found inspiration in the secret and subconscious. Emily Dickinson was known for how private her life was. Indeed, most of her life remained a mystery - what her inspirations were, who her lovers were." His voice got a little heavy at that last bit.

I then understood that this was to be a secret between me and Fred. *Something beautiful that we created just for ourselves, our own little book of poems,* he explained once, *What a lovely thing we share, my swan.* That was his name for me. I had no names for Fred.

If you wondered about Fred's wife, I did too. He assured me that she understood everything involving his poetry. We were not a religious type in that town. There was no priest keeping us accountable. We had too many worries with the weather, farming, and illness to be strict about morals.

***

Despite Fred's given purpose for fucking me, my poetry never came from these sessions. I never even wrote about Fred. Mostly, I wrote about myself. I think this bothered him. I wrote about a lover I hadn't met yet. When I thought of this lover, I felt nothing but light, like when you submerge underwater for the first time in the summer and rediscover the natural buoyancy of the human body. I wrote about the miracle of rose buds blooming in the winter - something I'd actually see every time the frost came; there was a patch of wood and concrete far down the road from home where two small roses always bloomed. I wrote about the pink expanse of the sky reflected on the water by the woods across the street. I wrote about my cat. I wrote about how I felt when my sister and I would climb the rooftop at night, after our parents had fallen asleep, and we watched the stars and moon over the fields. I loved poetry because it gave me language for how I noticed the world. Whenever that deadness in my gut weighed heavier, a poem helped me carry it better.

***

On that rainy afternoon, I had on a linen purple dress and fresh sandals with mustard-colored straps. The dress, which I had really loved when I sat in the sunny fields watching the last flowers of the season in full bloom, suddenly felt too short and uncomfortable as soon as Fred got here. I felt gaudy and exposed, and I felt a need to change. This was hardly rain-walking attire. But we hoped the rain had subsided by now.

We opened the door and Fred chivalrously opened an umbrella, but it was useless - the wind and rain beat down relentlessly. However, the garden out front always looked beautiful during the late summer rains. The greens were deeply greener. There were orange and red flowers. The remaining swans, drenched and not in the mood to attack any more, even added to the loveliness. But I couldn't look at the swans without holding something against them now.

"Be careful the cat doesn't get out!" someone yelled. But it was too late. The cat ran outside, her favorite way to misbehave, and into the rain. She hesitated and seemed confused. That seemed hopeful, that she would run back inside and save us the trouble of going into the rain to find her hiding by some muddy bush. But before she could turn around, a gust of wind blew her up into the sky and landed her on the roof and into the gutter. I watched her turn from large, round cat into a dove into a sparrow into finally a tiny white mouse. The mouse couldn't hold its own in the flooded gutter and flailed. "Cover the drain! Cover the drain!" I yelled.

But it was too late. I watched the white and pink body fall down through the drain and then disappear into the water. She would surely drown in minutes.

"She's dead." I looked at my dad, who had also seen the whole thing.

He looked empty. "We don't know that yet. Maybe not." He, finally, however, met my eyes and seeing my face, he softened. "Here come inside, don't go out today. Just stay by yourself and drink some tea in bed. I'll ask Fred for the books and maybe he can write a letter explaining them to you." My dad patted my shoulder.

Before going back inside, I watched more rain water pour down the drain. The first thing I felt had nothing to do with the cat. I felt relief. I wouldn't have to walk with Fred today.

UNTITLED.
Ashish Kumar Singh

The power of language, I have been told by a teacher,
is to make things exist. Name it, and it's there.

When I was fourteen, I didn't know what to call myself,
what attributes to attach and wear around my neck,

went through my days being unknown flying object.
How anything we didn't know was suddenly unknown,

its only identity our lack of language. I was
unlike other boys, lanky, un-sporty, my voice shrill,

hands literal wings flapping in panic. At the age
where every conversation turns to tits and pussies,

I'd nothing in my mouth except air in the shape of
a name and a slight tinge for muscles. It's a miracle

how you never find yourself but is found, named,
how I discovered myself by being still, letting them

unearth me like a piece of Harappan figurine,
giving me their mouths only to call myself a faggot.

THINGS I KNOW I LOVE MOST ABOUT HIM.

Ashish Kumar Singh

I could have made a list but grandma always says
love demands special gesture so instead I'm writing this.
A poem in his memory. A memoriam
not because he is dead or anything like that
but because he is alive and not with me.
I love his lanky frame, his too long legs,
his 3am snores, his large toes,
his mouth and my name inside it.
God forbid, if my grandma sees this.
She would say *what a 21-year-old know about love?*
Well, maybe not about love granny
but definitely about him.
I love when his nose turns red in cold,
his hands and short ears,
his hair on his chest, the mole just below the jaw
so faint one might miss it.
I love when he invites me to his rented room,
his giggle when he smuggles me out in the early morning.
She says *I never knew love, I knew duty*
because that's what my grandmother knew.
Now I know, and I want you to know that I know,
that I am the break in this heritage of not knowing.
Your own grandson, granny! I love him, and I know.

IT'S WINTER AND MY FATHER HAS FOUND OUT.

Ashish Kumar Singh

It's winter and my father has found out.
He says,
    choose son. This-
he waves his hands,
encompassing everything Home
    or that,
        meaning men, dirt, faggotry
        and probably death.
I'm 19 and
know the world only through films
    and bike rides with Ray.
My mother keeps on crying
even though the beating has stopped.
My feet look red
    and my hands tremble a little.
I'm so afraid my heart skips a beat.
I don't want to be out and
    alone in the cold.
So I choose to stay
    because I know,
    not everything you leave

will want you back.

ICARUS SYNDROME

Ashish Kumar Singh

Isn't it heroism   to go to a war
knowing there's no coming back?
I try
        in my own ways to do things
        that are daring.
Once
I took a bite of an unwashed apple
without my father knowing
or the time
        when I licked ice-cream
        off my fingers in public.
Everyday
at the risk of being outed
                      I look at him
through the iron chain-links
of the football field
like someone obsessed
        with their own reflection
                in the water.

I have always been discreet
at doing things
        I'm not suppose to do and
isn't that what makes us human
this urge
to break free like a wild fox on fire,
              touching everything
lighting the houses
              as you sprint through?
Didn't his father

                Daedalus warn him,
not to fly too close to the sun?
He did anyway, he dared
                and you might say
look what happened to the poor thing.

Like Icarus I want courage
because that's all it takes
        to tell him that he is the god
        the sun I wish to touch
whatever the cost
a push   a punch   a kick?
And if I get lucky, imagine the reward

                a nod, a smile, a kiss!

TWO TRUTHS AND A LIE

Kristen Zory King

Callie didn't have a tragedy of her own so she collected others, keeping them in her pocket and running her fingers against each scissored edge until they were so familiar by touch, so worn to the warmth of her fingertips, that she could almost believe they were hers. There were the obvious, daily ones, pulled out for sympathy at parties: the divorced parents or vague childhood trauma, the family dog run over in front of her very eyes, his insides pink as Pepto through clumped, matted fur. These were great for warm basements with half-burned Christmas lights and shitty cheap beer, when hardly anyone was listening to her anyway. She didn't need to add much detail, these stories already familiar in their suburban haze. She saved the good ones for special occasions, for the professors whose attention shifted, always, towards the pointed breasts and delicate wrists of girls in class, the boys who would make excuses to leave immediately after she blew them in her car, the heat from their bodies still smeared against the windows. When they would start checking their phones, the time, or when the conversation returned over and over to the classes they shared together, to grades or weather or football, she'd sigh and pull one out, something like: *you remind me of my brother. He passed away a few years ago. He was at a party, drank too much. Our neighbor found him belly-down in her pool the next morning.* She liked to watch the words as they left her mouth, wormed their way into someone else's brain, liked the way the boys blinked hard, twice, the carefully saved secret taking them away, if only for a moment, from themselves. Made them feel a soft lick of fear on their necks, understand how scared they should be, of the world, of her, of this stupid fucking town, of never getting out. I don't remember the first woe she told me, tinny and artificial, too pedestrian to stick, but I do remember the last one about best friends and forever and never being farther than a phone call. There were only two honest things about Callie: her loneliness and her blonde hair, which she wore long and, from the shine of it, had never been dyed. But I loved her anyway, slipping my tongue between her teeth even when she asked me not to, said our kisses weren't anything but a way to pass the time.

DEAD RINGER

Kristen Zory King

She couldn't quite make sense of it, but Alice was sure she saw herself standing on the corner of 17th and Ivy. It had been happening for a few days now: she'd be taking the dog for a walk, or standing in line at the bank, or driving to grab fresh basil, the one, crucial item that Ben had forgotten from the grocery store (honestly, why did she even bother with a list?), when her heart would stall in her chest, forgetting its steady rhythm as she saw herself standing just beyond. It wasn't a reflection, it was really her—her hair, cut in the way that framed her face and cost so much that she alternated credit cards each appointment; her shoulders, rolled back and down at the insistence of Jared, her personal trainer; her expensive, retro-style clogs, the ones she'd bought at the outlet in Albany three years ago, on one of those spring days that made her understand what the poet meant when she spoke of the thing with feathers, each bud around her standing sharp and primed to burst, seeking heat outside itself. Alice had once heard a woman on the radio say that women should buy clothing they found *aspirational,* remembered the girls from highschool, nipples pert through soft, worn t-shirts, wooden heels peeking from flared jeans like a wink, and felt a brief moment of, well, not joy but maybe relief, as she paid the cashier in cash, the shoes swinging from a plastic bag on her wrist. In truth, she never wore them. They were heavy and made her ankles sore. They didn't match her black tights or silk blouses. But she liked to keep them at the front of her closet, liked the idea that one day, she would be the kind of woman who wore them. Perhaps that's what the radio had meant, that she should *aspire* to be weightless and free with the possibility of youth, that at any moment, she could skip second period, play hooky under the open blue sky, kiss a jock under the bleachers. That she could roll down the front windows in her car, feel it shake from the hum of her favorite song. That her hair could tangle with the smell of bonfire. That her neck could be purpled in hickies. That she could stop running her tongue over memories and hopes that lived in her mouth like a tooth grown sore and rotten with age. Leaning toward the windshield, Alice made to get a better look at the doppelganger in front of her, surprised herself as the slight weight of her chest prompted a timid honk from the horn in her steering wheel. With a start, Alice's foot left the brake and she rolled into the car ahead of her, not hard enough to hurt, just to raise the insurance premium. Ben would be furious, though at least that would give him something to do. As Alice exchanged numbers with the driver (*really, so sorry, just lost myself for a moment there I guess, so glad no one was hurt*), she looked around for herself but found the street empty, not a trace remaining of the other woman with ripe flesh over sharp bones, shoulders relaxed and hips balanced in high, timbered heels. Only the sun moving slowly against another afternoon.

HUNGER MOON—
BEE LB

i'll turn my problems into pearls, ring them
around my neck; a noose beautiful enough
to inspire choking. my fingers inspiring

much the same. my tongue lolls. my lips
beg. words drip from my mouth,
spit slick and wounded.

could i unfurl the love i've made for you?
unwind the strings i've tied my heart with,
pull the beating mass back into my own body.

you said *bloom* and i spread. you said *bite*
and i filled. you said *bright* and i ate the light
of the hunger moon — i did not apologize.

licked the moon clean from its reflection in the lake.
bit each shine from the sky. you filled me
with some new kind of hunger. so i swallowed

the moon, a pearl hung in the night sky, a problem
i don't care to solve. planted it in the soft behind my
ribs; cage cradle, only the best for the problems at hand.

you gave ache to my bones. gave stretch to my need
til it filled the whole sky. jaw sore from all the pleasure
fit in my mouth. tonguing the wet skin til it split

into wound. tonguing some more to fit ache into want.

the light now dimmed from within my endless mouth,
the moon hung low and shuddered without.

i beg *more*, lips dripping pleas of starvation.
the touch of another. the weight of a body.
the hollow filled with night's light

filled with hope, hardy wonder multiplying across my body
shining so bright i could reflect the moon's light
had i not swallowed it down as my own.

the back bows. the knees curl. no apology will spill
toward devotion. night unfolds itself into day.
moon rolls around in my belly.

pearl forms beneath tongue, spat out as a
plea; my problem-pearl sits on the body
of the lake like a moon.

CONTRIBUTORS

Caroline Bock is the author of *Carry Her Home*, winner of the Fiction Award from the Washington Writers' Publishing House, and *LIE* and *Before My Eyes*, young adult novels, from St. Martin's Press. The winner of the 2018 *Writer* magazine story award and the 2021 Adrift story award from Driftwood Press, she is also the fiction editor of the anthology *This Is What America Looks Like: poetry and fiction from DC, Maryland, and Virginia* and co-editor of the literary journal *WWPH Writes*. Her creative work has appeared in *SmokeLong, Ploughshares, Bethesda Magazine, Brevity, Gargoyle, the Grace & Gravity series* and more. In 2011, she earned an MFA in Fiction from The City College of New York. Find her often at Twitter at cabockwrites.

(Letitia Despina)
1984 born
wrote
2008 moved to dk
wrote
2009-2010 lived in delhi
wrote...
2014 became mother
2015 graduated MA film/media
2020-2021 aged a lot, **even though time compressed**
2021 (at the very end)—published first volume of pohetry (which also has *shit* in the title)

Meg Eden is a 2020 Pitch Wars mentee, and teaches creative writing at Anne Arundel Community College. She is the author of the 2021 Towson Prize for Literature winning poetry collection "Drowning in the Floating World" (Press 53, 2020) and children's novels, most recently "Selah's Guide to Normal" (Scholastic, 2023). Find her online at www.megedenbooks.com or on Twitter at @ConfusedNarwhal and Instagram at @meden_author.

Taiwo Hassan is a writer of Yorùbá descent, a poet and a vocalist. A Best Of The Net Nominee, his poems have appeared in trampset, Kissing Dynamite, Lucent Dreaming, The Shore, Brittle Paper, Dust Poetry Magazine, Ice Floe Press, Wizards In Space and several other places. He emerged the first runner-up for the MANI 10 year anniversary Poetry Competition. He's also an undergraduate student of Demography and Social Statistics at Obafemi Awolowo University, Ilé-Ifè, Osun State, Nigeria. His first chapbook, Birds Don›t Fly For Pleasure is forthcoming for publication by River Glass Books.

Kristen Zory King is a writer and teaching artist based in Washington, DC. Recent work can be found in Electric Lit, The Citron Review, Tiny Molecules, Emerge Literary Journal, and mac(ro)mic, among others. She is currently working on a collection of flash fiction and micro stories. Learn more or be in touch at **www.kristenzoryking.com**.

BEE LB is an array of letters, bound to impulse; they are a writer creating delicate connections. they have called any number of places home; currently, a single yellow wall in Michigan. they have been published in Revolute Lit, Roanoke Review, After the Pause, and corporeal, among others. they are a poetry reader for Capsule Stories.

A.C. Mandelbaum is an ex-philosopher with a day job who lives in Seattle.

Tiffany Promise (she/her) is a writer, poet, chronic migraineur, and the mother of two wildlings. She holds an MFA from CalArts, and her work has been published/forthcoming in Narrative Magazine, Brevity, Creative Nonfiction, Trnsfr, Okay Donkey and elsewhere. Tiffany now lives in Austin, Texas, but is originally from the mudbug-riddled swelter of the Gulf Coast, which is the setting of her first novel, Eggs.

Corinna Schulenburg (she/her) is a queer trans artist/activist committed to ensemble practice and social justice. She's a mother, a playwright, a poet, and a Creative Partner of Flux Theatre Ensemble. Poems in: *Arachne Press, Beaver Magazine, Capsule Stories, Lost Pilots, Long Con, LUPERCALIA Press, miniskirt magazine, Moist, Moonflake Press, Moss*

Puppy, Oroboro, Okay Donkey, Poet Lore, SHIFT, The Shore, The Westchester Review, and more. https://corinnaschulenburg.com/writer/poet/

Stuti Sharma is a poet, stand up comic, and photographer. You can find her in the prairies of Illinois or eating at restaurants where cooks facetime their family. She believes love is the most powerful force in the world. You can see more of her work and contact her at cyborgstuti.weebly.com.

Ashish Kumar Singh (he/him) is a queer poet from India and a post graduate student of English Literature. Other than writing, he reads and sleeps extensively. Previously, his works have been published in Chestnut Review, Blue Marble Review, Brave New Voices etc.

Debra Stone's poetry, essays and fiction can be found in *Under the Gum Tree, Random Sample Review, Green Mountains Review (GMR), About Place Journal, Saint Paul Almanac, Wild Age Press, Gyroscope, Tidal Basin*, and forthcoming in other literary journals. Sundress Publishers nominated Debra's essay, *Grandma Essie's Vanilla Poundcake*, Best of the Net, judged by Hanif Abdurraquib in 2019. In 2021 her poem, *year-of- staying–in place*, was nominated Best of the Net and Pushcart nominated. She's received residencies at the Vermont Studio Center, Callaloo, The Anderson Center for Interdisciplinary Studies, New York Mills Arts Residency and is a Kimbilio Fellow. In 2019 she was a Loft Fellow for the Minnesota based The Loft Mentor Series in creative nonfiction and was a finalist for The Loft Emerging Writers Grant. She is also a recipient of a Minnesota State Arts Board Cultural Community Partnership Grant and Minnesota Regional Arts Council Grant. Debra is Vice-chair and Chair of the Governance Committee at Graywolf Press in Minneapolis.

Morgan Ziegenhorn (she/they) is a graduate of UC Berkeley with a degree in biology and a minor in creative writing. Her work has previously appeared in 805 Literature and Arts, You Might Need to Hear This, and Persephone's Daughters. She recently earned her PhD. from Scripps Institution of Oceanography studying the voices and behaviors of whales and dolphins. She is from Sacramento, California.

CPSIA information can be obtained
at www.ICGtesting.com
Printed in the USA
JSHW050946240822
29561JS00004B/21